THE PUPPY PLACE

COCOA

THE PUPPY PLACE

Don't miss any of these
other stories by Ellen Miles!

THE PUPPY PLACE

COCOA

ELLEN MILES

SCHOLASTIC INC.

New York   Toronto   London   Auckland
Sydney   Mexico City   New Delhi   Hong Kong

For Sarah B. and Toby

ISBN 978-0-545-34835-5

Cover art by Tim O'Brien
Original cover design by Steve Scott

12 11 10 9 8 7 6 5   13 14 15 16/0

Printed in the U.S.A.   40

First printing, December 2011

CHAPTER ONE

"And veggie lo mein! Don't forget the veggie lo mein for Mom!" Charles tugged on his dad's sleeve as they turned the corner. They were on their way to China Star, the Peterson family's favorite takeout place.

"How could we forget the veggie lo mein?" Dad asked. "Mom would kill me. And Lizzie would be furious if we forgot the spring rolls."

Charles grinned. "Shrimp, not pork," he sang out, mimicking his older sister. "And what about the Bean's Special Chicken?" His younger brother, whose real name was Adam, adored a certain chicken dish on China Star's menu. The Bean thought it was named Special Chicken, since that's what Mom called it when she put some on his plate, but its real name was General Tso's.

Dad nodded. "We won't forget that. And of course, I'm ordering the beef with broccoli. What about you?" he asked, as he pulled open China Star's door.

Charles stepped inside. A sudden blast of steamy, fragrant air surrounded him. It was cold outside, but the restaurant was warm and bright and bustling. Friday night was always a busy night at China Star. People stood in line, looking up at the menu board above the counter. Behind the counter was an open kitchen, where three men worked at a fast, steady pace. They stirred ingredients in big, round woks over the leaping flames of two gigantic stoves, shouting to one another and to the counter person as they worked.

Charles loved coming to China Star. The usual routine was that he and Dad drove downtown, ordered the food, and then stopped in at the firehouse where Dad worked. They'd visit there for a few minutes until their food was ready, then pick it up and drive home quickly. Lizzie and Mom would have the table all set, and moments later the whole family would be sighing happily as they filled their plates and dug into the delicious food. Buddy, the Petersons' puppy, would sit under the table waiting hopefully for a scrap to fall on the floor. China Star night was always a good night.

There was only one problem. Charles wished he had a favorite dish, like everybody else in the family. Every time he came to China Star, he would stare up at the brightly lit menu, trying to puzzle out which item to order. The picture of shrimp wo bar always made his mouth water, but he had tried it once and it was greasy and gross. He liked the sound of sing ding snow dim, but his dad had warned him that it would probably be too spicy for him. He had tried sweet and sour pork, moo shu chicken, and beef chop suey, and they were all good. But he wasn't quite ready to name any of them as his favorite.

Fortunately, there were three people ahead of them in line, so Charles had a little time to think.

Unfortunately, the line moved very quickly.

"Yes?" The woman at the counter looked at Dad, waiting for his order.

"Beef with broccoli, please," Dad said. "And shrimp spring rolls, one order, and vegetable lo mein, and General Tso's chicken. And . . ." He looked at Charles.

Charles panicked. He had been trying to decide between moo goo gai pan, egg foo young, and chicken chow mein, but none of them seemed exactly right. The woman was waiting, pen in hand. Dad was waiting. The customers in line behind them were waiting. He glanced up at the menu again and blurted out, "House Special chow fun!" which was the first thing his eye fell on.

"Are you sure?" Dad asked.

Charles nodded.

"Okay, then," Dad said.

The woman at the counter rang up their order and Dad paid. "Twenty minutes," she told them, as she spun around to hand the order to one of the cooks.

When they turned to go, Charles spotted a tall, skinny guy who'd been standing in line a few places behind them. "Harry!" he said.

"Hey there, man," said Harry, grinning at Charles as he held up a hand for a high five. "What's up?"

Charles beamed back at Harry. "The sky," he said, as he smacked Harry's hand. "The sky is up."

Harry let out a huge guffaw, and Charles laughed, too. Harry was such a cool guy. He was a baseball and basketball star at the high school. He drove a rusty old red convertible. He had the coolest dog, a big chocolate Lab named Zeke who always wore a red bandana. And he went out with Dee, a really nice girl who also happened to have a chocolate Lab. Murphy was Dee's service dog, and he was so smart. Since Dee got around in a wheelchair, Murphy helped her in a million ways. He could pick up anything she dropped, for example, or help her put on her socks.

Harry nodded at Dad. "Are you guys fostering a puppy these days?" he asked.

Harry knew that the Peterson family fostered puppies, which meant that they took care of puppies who needed homes — just until they could find each one the perfect forever family. In fact, Charles had first met Harry when the Peterson family was fostering a very spoiled Yorkie named Princess.

"Nope," said Dad. "We're a one-puppy household for the time being."

"Buddy doesn't mind getting all the attention," Charles added.

"Hey, would you like to join us for dinner?" Dad asked Harry. "We just ordered enough food for an army."

Harry smiled. "I'd love to, but I can't. I'm ordering a bunch of stuff to bring to a meeting over at city hall. I'm on the WinterFest committee and we've got a lot of work to do before next week."

WinterFest happened every year in Littleton, around the holidays. It took place on the playing fields at Charles and Lizzie's school. There were snow sculptures, a relay race, all kinds of games, and hot cocoa and singing around a bonfire at the end of the afternoon. "That's right!" Charles said. "WinterFest is next Saturday! I love WinterFest."

"So do I," said Harry. "Which is a good thing, since Dee is head of the planning committee this year. She talked me into working on it, and we've been having a blast thinking up new games and activities." Harry looked at Charles. "Hey, you want to be on my relay race team? Our name is Rudolph's Revenge, and we need a third person."

Charles stared at Harry. "Me?"

Harry shrugged. "Sure, why not? You'd be great."

"Well — okay!" Charles felt his face grow hot with the pleasure of being asked. He wasn't really the racing type, but he couldn't help saying yes. He would have agreed to just about anything if it meant hanging out with Harry, the coolest guy he knew.

"Oops, guess it's my turn to order," said Harry, stepping up to the counter. "I'll call you, okay, Charles?"

"Okay!" Charles waved as he followed Dad to the door.

Dad's phone beeped as they were leaving the restaurant. He pulled it out and frowned down at it. "Seven text messages?" he asked. "Nobody ever texts me." He read silently for a moment. "Hmmm," he said. "Interesting."

"What do they say?" Charles asked.

"They're from Meg, at the firehouse," Dad said. Meg Parker was a firefighter, just like Dad. "She wants us to get over there as fast as we can."

"Is it an emergency?" Charles asked, as they hustled down the street toward the firehouse. Clouds of white mist puffed from his mouth as he talked, and he banged his hands together to warm them up. It sure was cold!

"Not exactly," said Dad. "It's about a puppy."

CHAPTER TWO

"A puppy?" Charles felt his heart skip a beat. "What about a puppy?"

"I'm trying to figure that out." Dad stopped on the sidewalk, staring at the screen of his phone. "These messages are all jumbled. Meg seems to be trying to tell me that —"

"Dad!" Charles tugged on his father's sleeve.

"Hold on, bucko," Dad said, still toggling away at his phone. "Let me just —"

"But Dad, look! Isn't that Meg? With that dog?" Charles pointed up the street. A big, strong dog dragged a woman toward them, pulling her like a boat tows a water-skier. Charles noticed the dog's beautiful brown coat and thought that it must be a chocolate Lab, because it looked just like Zeke and Murphy, Harry's and Dee's dogs.

"Yeeeooww!" yelled Meg. "Sorry! Sorry!" she said to the other people on the sidewalk, as she ran along behind the dog, barely missing a lamppost, a mailbox, and a fire hydrant.

Dad had finally let his phone fall to his side, and he stared openmouthed as Meg and the dog charged closer. "I guess that must be the puppy she was writing about," he said.

"Here, pup," said Charles, as the dog approached. He squatted down and held his arms open and the dog barreled into him, knocking him over. Then, as Charles lay laughing on the sidewalk, the dog licked every part of his face: his chin, his mouth, his cheeks, his nose, his closed eyes, his forehead, and his ears. Charles laughed even harder because it tickled so much. When he opened his eyes, he saw the dog standing over him, grinning a doggy grin and panting happily.

Her big thick tail bashed Dad in the knees with every wag.

"This is a *puppy*?" Dad asked Meg, as he bent to pat the dog's head.

Meg laughed. "Well, yes. She's only about a year old. But I have a feeling this dog will be *acting* like a puppy for a long, long time."

"She's beautiful," said Charles. He threw his arms around the dog's strong neck and kissed her silky soft ears. Her glossy coat was the exact color of a Kit Kat, Charles's favorite chocolate bar. But she didn't smell like chocolate. She smelled like dog, which was even better. Her yellowish eyes were bright, her ears were alert, and her brown nose twitched and shivered, working overtime to sniff out all the good downtown smells. She had long, gangly legs and huge, chunky paws, and she was at least twice as big as Buddy. "What's her name?" he asked Meg.

"Cocoa," said Meg.

When the dog heard her name, she whirled around and jumped up excitedly onto Meg, making her stagger backward into Dad. "Whoa, there," Dad said, as he helped Meg stand upright again. "This dog sure does have a lot of energy."

Charles squatted on the sidewalk and tried to calm Cocoa down. He gave her nice, long pats the whole length of her body. That usually worked for Buddy when he was overexcited.

"Tell me about it," said Meg, sighing. "That's why we need to find her a home — fast. I already have my hands full with my two dogs. I can't handle this one, too."

"A home?" Dad asked.

Charles felt his heart skip another beat. Maybe Cocoa was going to be their next foster puppy!

"Didn't you get my texts?" Meg said.

"I was just trying to read them, but I couldn't quite —"

Meg waved a hand. "I know. I was kind of in a hurry. Anyway, here's the story. This pup belongs to an older couple, Ernest and Charlotte Thayer, out on Franklin Street."

"Judge Thayer?" Dad asked.

"That's right, he used to be a judge. He's retired now. He and his wife are both pretty frail, but they still manage to live in their own house and take care of themselves."

Charles wasn't sure what "frail" meant, but he had a feeling it was the opposite of the way Cocoa was.

"And?" Dad asked.

"And a couple of hours ago, the dog came running toward Ernest, banged into him hard, and knocked him over," Meg finished, all in a rush. "I was one of the EMTs on the call, and it was obvious that Charlotte was not going to be able to take care of this puppy on her own. Anyway, Charlotte came with us in the ambulance, so there wasn't going to be anybody at home with the dog, so —"

"So you brought Cocoa along, too?" Dad asked.

Cocoa's head snapped up when she heard her name, but Charles still had his arms around her, so she didn't jump onto Dad. "Good girl, good girl," he whispered into her ear.

Meg nodded. "She rode right up front in the ambulance, with Ted. I couldn't figure out any other way to deal with the problem. And now —"

Dad made a face. "I get it. Now you want us to take this crazy mutt."

"She's not a mutt, Dad!" Charles burst out. "She's a beautiful purebred chocolate Lab, just like Zeke and Murphy, and she's a good girl, at least she could *learn* to be a good girl, and we *have* to take her, we just *have* to!"

Dad smiled down at Charles. He sighed. He reached out a hand to pat Cocoa's glossy head. "I guess you're right. We do have to. Cocoa needs somewhere to stay, at least until Judge Thayer is out of the hospital." He reached for the phone he'd stowed in his pocket. "I'll call your mom to make sure it's all right with her. Then we'd better go back to China Star to pick up our food, before it gets cold!"

Charles hugged Cocoa. "Yay!" he whispered into her ear. "You're coming home with us."

CHAPTER THREE

"Whooaaa!" Charles let out a whoop as Cocoa towed him down the sidewalk, the same way she'd towed Meg. This sure was one strong puppy. It wasn't easy to get her to sit still outside of China Star while Dad went in to pick up their food, but Charles tried his best. "Sit, Cocoa," he said. Instead of sitting, the dog jumped up on him, her big paws landing squarely in the middle of his chest.

That's my name! That's my name! That's my name!

Charles staggered, but did not fall down. He tried to remember what Lizzie, who knew everything about training dogs, would say about what to do next. "Ignore the bad behavior and reward good behavior," she always said. So Charles did not yell at Cocoa or touch her or say her name again. He just turned to one side so that her paws slid off him and she landed back on the sidewalk.

"Sit," he said again. This time he didn't use her name, since he could already see that hearing her name always seemed to make Cocoa very excited. And this time, he put his hand on her butt, pressing gently but firmly to make sure she understood what he wanted. At the same moment, he pulled up a little on the leash so that her head came up as her butt went down. He resisted the urge to say "sit" again, remembering that it never helped to repeat a command over and over. He'd learned all of this when he and Lizzie had taken one of their foster puppies, a wild Jack Russell terrier named Rascal, to puppy kindergarten.

"Good *girl!*" Charles cried when Cocoa sat. Immediately, she sprang up again and danced around him, wriggling her whole body and grinning a big doggy grin.

Yay, yay, yay! I made you happy!

"Oh, boy," sighed Charles as he untangled the leash and got ready to start over.

"Hey, wow!" Harry came out of China Star carrying a shopping bag loaded with food. "Is this the puppy your dad just told me about? She looks exactly like Zeke when he was a pup." He set the bag on the sidewalk and knelt down, opening his arms to Cocoa. "Oh, you. Oh, you silly girl. Oh, yes, you're a knucklehead, aren't you?" he murmured, as he let her lick him all over his face. Then he snatched up the bag before she could stick her nose into it. He grinned at Charles.

"You're going to have your hands full with this one," he said. "I guarantee it."

"I know," said Charles, shaking his head. "But she's going to be a great dog. I can already tell."

"I'll come visit her one day soon," said Harry. "And we'll talk more about the relay race, okay?" He held out his hand for a high five.

Charles smacked his hand. "Okay," he said.

Harry began to walk toward city hall. "Hey," he called, turning back toward Charles. "You do know how to cross-country ski, right?"

"Well . . ." Charles began. He had tried cross-country skiing exactly once, when his family had gone on a winter vacation in Vermont. He'd loved it, and he had seemed to pick it up more quickly than Lizzie, but he couldn't exactly claim to be an expert. He did have his own skis, though. Dad had gotten them at a ski swap in the fall. "Yeah, I guess I do."

"Great!" said Harry. "See ya!" With a wave, he jogged off.

Charles watched him go, wondering what he had gotten himself into.

A few minutes later, Dad came out of the restaurant. "Let's go," he said.

Cocoa didn't need any encouragement to jump into Dad's pickup. She seemed to be happy to do whatever Charles and Dad asked her to do. Charles thought that might be a good sign. Maybe she would be a quick learner. Charles hugged her close as they drove home. His mouth watered as the spicy smells of China Star food filled the cab of the truck.

Lizzie threw open the door as soon as they pulled into the driveway. "Where is she? Oh, she's adorable! Come here, Cocoa!"

Cocoa leapt out of the truck and charged toward Lizzie before Charles could grab her leash. "Oof!" Lizzie gasped as Cocoa jumped up onto her. She sat down hard on the back steps, laughing as Cocoa licked her face all over.

"That's how she says hello," Charles said. "She's a big kisser."

"She's pretty big, period," said Lizzie, throwing her arms around the puppy. "You're a big, goofy girl, that's what."

"Better make sure she doesn't knock the Bean over, or jump up on Mom," warned Dad. "That wouldn't be a good start."

"I'll take her out in the backyard for a minute and let her run around," suggested Charles. "Maybe she'll burn off some energy."

Out back, Charles discovered that Cocoa was very good at playing fetch. He threw Buddy's ratty old tennis ball for her over and over. Cocoa scrambled for the ball, racing after it and catching it on the second or third bounce, every time. Then she dashed back to Charles, grinning around the tennis ball clenched tight in her jaws. She dropped it at his feet, then backed up to wait, eyes shining and tail wagging, until he picked it up and threw it again.

"Okay," said Charles, after a while. "I'm starving, and my arm hurts. Time to go in." Cocoa sat and cocked her head at him.

Now? Just when we were starting to have fun?

Charles laughed. "We'll play more tomorrow," he promised. Cocoa galloped up the back porch stairs and followed him inside.

"Yum," said Charles when he came into the kitchen. Mom had set all the food out on the table, and it looked great — especially the House Special chow fun, with its wide noodles and mixture of veggies, shrimp, and meat. Cocoa dashed past him, put her muddy paws up on the counter, and grabbed an empty take-out container in her jaws.

"No!" yelled Mom. "Bad dog."

Startled, Cocoa let the container fall from her mouth. She ambled over to the water dish Mom had set out and lapped noisily, splashing water all over the floor. Then she walked around in a circle three times, landed with a thump on the floor, and fell asleep almost instantly.

"We're going to have to do some extra puppy-proofing in this house, I can see that," said Mom, shaking her head. But she was smiling. Cocoa was too cute to be mad at for long.

CHAPTER FOUR

The House Special chow fun was delicious. Charles loved the big wide noodles and the yummy sauce. Maybe he had finally found his favorite dish.

Cocoa was still sleeping when the Petersons finished dinner. Quickly, Dad cleared the table while Lizzie and Charles helped Mom to puppy-proof the house. They put away anything a curious dog might lick or eat or chew. They locked the garbage in the garage, and put the dog biscuits up in one of the high cabinets that only Mom and Dad could reach. They closed the bathroom doors so Cocoa wouldn't get into the soap or the toilet paper, and they tucked their most favorite books into their bookshelves. They didn't have to do all this work for every puppy they fostered, or for Buddy, who was very well trained by now. But everybody remembered Jack, the boxer pup they had fostered, who had eaten — well, he'd eaten everything he could get his teeth into, basically. Including one of Lizzie's most treasured books.

Cocoa raced around the house when she woke up, sniffing here and snuffling there. Charles loved to watch the way she got to know this new place. She was friendly to Buddy and she licked the Bean all over his face, making him laugh his googly laugh. She took every single toy out of Buddy's toy basket and left them strewn all over the living room, but at least she didn't tear any of them up. Then, after she ate her own dinner, she lay down on the bed they had put out for her and went back to sleep.

For the rest of the weekend, the Petersons made sure that Cocoa was never alone. Charles and Lizzie walked her and threw balls for her and played games with her, keeping her busy. Plus, she played with Buddy.

Buddy loved Cocoa. From the second they met, they were like best friends. They even looked as if they might be related, despite the way the long-legged Lab towered over the smaller brown pup. They played all the time, every minute that they were both awake. They raced around the house, chasing each other. They played tug with Buddy's toys. They wrestled on the living room rug. And when Charles took them outside they galloped around happily, chasing balls and each other and barking at squirrels.

By Sunday afternoon, Cocoa had already begun to calm down — a little. Charles decided that this was a good time to teach her a few things, especially since Dad and Lizzie had taken Buddy to the dog park to give him and Cocoa some time on their own.

Charles was in the living room, working on teaching Cocoa how to lie down on command, but he was having a hard time concentrating. The Bean had decided to practice his WinterFest songs in the same room. This year the Bean's preschool was going to be starting off the festival's caroling, and lately he went around singing all the time. Charles had never imagined that he could get tired of hearing "Deck the Halls," but now that he had heard it for the millionth time he was starting to think maybe he could.

"Deck the halls with bells of jolly," sang the Bean. He stood near the fireplace, holding his hands up in front of him like little paws. *"Fa la la la la, la la la la."*

Charles laughed. There was no point in correcting his little brother. The Bean could be very stubborn about things, and if he thought you decked halls with bells of jolly instead of boughs of holly, there would be no changing his mind. Anyway, Charles wasn't a hundred percent sure what a bough of holly really was, so he didn't want to get into a discussion about it.

"Deck the halls with bells of jolly," sang the Bean again. He was still holding up his little paws.

"What are you supposed to be," Charles asked. "A squirrel?"

The Bean made googly-eyes at him. "No, silly!" He tossed his head. "Didn't you see my antlers? I'm a reindeer! My whole class is reindeers!"

Sure enough, the Bean was wearing a headband that supported two velvety brown antlers, decorated with sparkly white snowflakes. "I *am* a silly," Charles admitted. "Those antlers are very cool. Can I try them on?"

The Bean hesitated, touching his antlers.

"Just for a few minutes?" Charles asked.

The Bean folded his arms, thinking about it.

"I'll let you play with my Legos," said Charles. "You can build anything you want. You can even use the wheel thingies."

The Bean smiled. "Okay," he said. He took off the headband and handed the antlers to Charles.

Charles put on the antlers, checking in the hall mirror to make sure they were adjusted just right. He grinned at himself. They looked pretty good. He liked the way they felt, too. He lifted his chin and squared his shoulders. He felt strong and . . . *noble*, that was the word. He felt noble. He could picture himself sailing through the air, pulling Santa's sleigh tirelessly all through the starry night.

The Bean had gone off to find Mom, so Charles kept the antlers on as he went back to working with Cocoa. If you could get her to calm down a little and focus, she really was a fast learner. He had played ball with her in the backyard for a long time that morning, so she wasn't quite as wild. It did not take long at all to teach her how to wait when they came to a door, to pause to let him go first instead of pushing her way through ahead of him. He practiced in the doorway between the hall and the living room.

When Charles held up a hand and said, "Wait," Cocoa sat — well, not quite, but she crouched — until he went through and said, "Okay!" Then she raced through the door to where he stood holding a treat. True, she usually raced past him, or into him, but so far she had not knocked him over. As soon as she'd gobbled each treat she spun around in circles, barking at Charles.

This is fun! Let's do it again.

"Okay, okay, calm down, Cocoa. Ready to try one more time?" Charles asked. But just as he was getting set for another round, he heard a knock at the door. Cocoa scrambled wildly over the wood floors, galloping to the door and screeching to a halt in front of it. She barked loudly.

Hurry up! Open the door! Open the door! Let's see who it is!

Charles peeked through the window. It was Harry! He had a girl with him, a tall, thin girl Charles did not know. Charles flung the door open. "Hey," he said happily.

Then he remembered.

He was still wearing the antlers.

CHAPTER FIVE

Charles put his hand up to the antlers, ready to pull them off. His face was hot with embarrassment. What would Harry and this girl think? Who went around wearing antlers?

Harry burst into laughter, and the girl next to him giggled.

Charles wanted to crawl under the hall table.

"Those are awesome," Harry said. "What a great idea!"

"Idea?" Charles could not quite believe his ears. Had Harry called the antlers "awesome"? "What do you mean?" He turned to Cocoa, who was dancing around happily, sniffing at first Harry's legs, then the girl's. "Easy, Cocoa," Charles said. "Take it easy."

"For part of our team costume," said Harry, reaching down to pet Cocoa. "They're perfect. Rudolph's Revenge, remember? That's our name. Of course we have to wear antlers." He stepped over to pluck the antlers off Charles's head. "May I?" he asked. He went over to the hall mirror and adjusted the headband so that the antlers stood tall and proud on his own head. "Oh, yeah!" he crowed. "Like I said. Perfect." He pulled them off and handed them to the girl. "Try them, Dawna."

But the girl had knelt down on the floor to say hello to Cocoa. The big brown pup wriggled with pleasure as the girl stroked her ears and scratched her head. "This dog is adorable," she said. "And she's so, so sweet. What a darling." Cocoa gave Dawna several huge licks, her tail wagging so hard that it banged the wall beside her.

"Oh!" said Harry. "I forgot to introduce you. Charles, this is Dawna. She's the other member of our team. We're really lucky to have her, too. Dawna is an Ironman athlete. Do you know what that means?"

Charles shook his head.

"It's nothing," said Dawna, rising to her feet. She smiled at Charles. "Good to meet you," she said, sticking out a hand. Cocoa barked a few times, then sat down and panted, putting a paw on Dawna's knee and whining for more attention.

Charles shook her hand, noticing that she had a very firm grip. "What's an Ironman?" he asked.

"It's just a race," said Dawna. She reached down to pet Cocoa. "Shh, girl," she said. "It's okay."

"Just a race!" Harry laughed. "Listen to this, Charles. It's a race where you have to swim almost two and a half miles, then ride your bike for a hundred and twelve miles, then run twenty-six miles. All in one day! It takes place in Hawaii every year. And last year Dawna was the world champion in her age group. She's amazing."

Dawna shrugged. "I got lucky," she said. "Some of the other top competitors had the flu."

Harry rolled his eyes.

"How do you even *do* that?" Charles asked. He could hardly imagine being able to do one of those things, much less all three in a single day.

"It's just a matter of training," said Dawna. "I'm a physical therapist — that means I help people strengthen their bodies — so I know all the tricks. I spend a couple of hours every day either biking or running or swimming, and on weekends I spend even more time. I like it, even though it gets a little lonesome and boring sometimes." She looked down at Cocoa, who had settled down a bit. Now the brown puppy was leaning against her leg, gazing up at her new friend lovingly as she waited for more pats. "Anyway, enough about me.

Tell me about this gorgeous pup. Where did you get her?"

"She's not ours," Charles said. "We're just fostering her, taking care of her because her owner got hurt. Actually, she ran into him and knocked him over. He had to go to the hospital."

"Not Judge Thayer!" said Dawna. "I know him! He's a patient of mine at the rehab center. I heard all about his crazy dog." She scratched Cocoa's head. "Don't you worry, honey," she murmured to the puppy. "He's not mad at you. It wasn't really your fault."

"That's where Dawna and I met," said Harry. "At the rehab center." He must have seen Charles's confused look, because he added, "Rehab is short for rehabilitation. It means a place where people go to get over injuries. Anyway, did I tell you that Zeke is a therapy dog now?" He grinned. "I'm so proud of him. And people just love him when I bring him to visit at the rehab place or the hospital."

Charles knew all about therapy dogs. They were specially trained dogs who were calm enough and friendly enough to be able to visit people who were sick or hurt. Patting a dog or watching a dog do tricks could really cheer someone up and maybe even help them heal faster. One of the puppies his family had fostered — Sweetie, a miniature poodle — was in training to be a therapy dog.

"Maybe I could bring Cocoa to visit Judge Thayer," Charles said. "Wouldn't he like that?"

Dawna didn't say anything for a moment. "Well," she said, "I think maybe Cocoa's a little too —"

Charles nodded. "I know. She's rambunctious."

Dawna laughed. "Great word," she said.

"It means energetic and kind of wild," said Charles, in case Dawna wasn't sure.

"That's Cocoa," said Dawna, looking fondly down at the big brown puppy, who was now prancing around in circles, chasing her own tail.

"But maybe you could come visit the judge and

tell him how Cocoa's doing," suggested Harry. "I'm taking Zeke over to the rehab place tomorrow afternoon. Want to come with me?"

"Sure!" Charles loved to ride in Harry's red sports car.

"So, anyway," Harry said, "we're here to talk about our team, right?"

"Right!" said Charles. He led them into the living room and they sat down. Cocoa immediately pounced on the toy basket and grabbed Mr. Duck. She chewed hard on him to make him squeak, and shook him in her jaws so that his wings flipped and flapped. Then she romped over to Dawna, eyes gleaming, and shoved Mr. Duck into her lap.

Isn't this a great toy? Don't you love it?

Dawna laughed. She took the toy and threw it for Cocoa. "You're always in motion, aren't you?"

she asked. Then she turned to Charles. "So, about the relay race. Harry tells me you're going to do the cross-country skiing part. I'm going to be the snowshoe runner, and Harry's doing the sled."

The WinterFest relay race always began with a member of each team flopping belly first onto a sled and racing down the long, steep hill above the school playground.

Harry saw the question on Charles's face before he could even ask it. "I'm doing the sled because I'm a disaster on cross-country skis and Dawna's a much faster runner than me."

Charles nodded. He just hoped *he* wouldn't be a disaster on cross-country skis.

"Now all we need is enough snow," said Dawna. "Remember two years ago, when they had to cancel the race? That was a bummer."

Charles nodded. Right now there was only a trace of snow on the ground. *Hmmm* . . . If the race was cancelled, he wouldn't have to worry about making a fool of himself on skis.

"The weather guy said we might get a little snow this afternoon and tonight," Harry said. They all turned to look out the big living room window. Charles gulped. The first big, white flakes had already begun to fall.

CHAPTER SIX

It snowed lightly all night, just enough to coat everything in a bright white blanket but not quite enough for school to be cancelled. It was still snowing by the time school ended. Charles helped Mom shovel the driveway, and they finished just as Harry came to pick him up for their visit to the rehab center. "This is a great start on the snow we need," said Harry, brushing the snow off his jacket as he came up the walk.

Charles nodded. "Great," he agreed, even though he still wasn't sure about this skiing thing.

Mom stood by the door, holding Cocoa so she wouldn't bolt outside. The Lab puppy and Buddy had already played in the backyard for hours that day. They were both crazy about the snow. "Does your car have snow tires?" Mom asked Harry, looking worried.

"Oh, sure," said Harry. "Good ones, too. Only the best for Stella."

"Stella?" Mom asked.

"That's my car's name," said Harry. "Dee came up with it. Anyway, my car goes really well in the snow," he assured her. "Charles will be totally safe, I promise." He turned to Charles. "Ready? Zeke's waiting out in the car."

"Ready," said Charles. He gave Cocoa a hug. "I'll tell Judge Thayer you said hello," he promised her.

Charles loved Harry's rusty old red convertible, but he had to admit that it was more fun to ride in it during the summer, when the top was down and everyone could see you driving past with the wind in your hair. Now that it was winter, the top was up — but it didn't really do much to keep things warm inside. The heater did not seem to work too well, either. Plus, Zeke kept trying to crawl into the front seat to sit in Charles's lap. Harry laughed. "He just wants to warm you up," he said as Charles tried to shove the big dog back into his own seat for the third time. Charles's feet felt like blocks of ice by the time Harry pulled into a parking spot at the rehab center.

Harry adjusted Zeke's red bandana, snapped on his leash, and led Charles inside. "This place is terrific," he said, as he signed them in at the front desk. "They work really hard with people here. You'll see." He walked down the hall, with Zeke walking nicely beside him. Charles was impressed with Zeke's good manners. Whenever they came up to a person, Zeke immediately sat and offered his paw.

At first, Charles felt a little shy. A lot of the people at the rehab place were in wheelchairs, or on crutches, or wrapped in bandages. But they all reacted to Zeke with smiles and pats and hugs. Everybody loved dogs, even when they were sick or injured.

Harry stopped in front of a room and peered inside. "I think this is Judge Thayer's room, but he doesn't seem to be in there," he said.

An aide passing by smiled as she patted Zeke's head. "He's probably down in the PT room," she said. "You know, physical therapy? He spends a lot of time in there every day."

"I know where that is," Harry said. He headed down to the end of the hall and pushed through double doors into a large, brightly lit room. Charles looked around. The PT room was set up like a gym. It was full of people doing all kinds of interesting things with different equipment: tossing giant balls back and forth, pulling on colorful oversized rubber bands, walking between parallel bars, and riding on exercise bikes.

"Look who's here." Harry pointed to Dawna, who was helping a tall, thin man step up onto and back down from a wooden box. Like most of the other patients, he was dressed in sweatpants and a pajama top. But there was something about the way he held himself that made him seem as if he were wearing a suit and tie and polished shoes.

"Hey!" said Dawna. "Here they are, Judge." She introduced Harry and Charles. "This is Judge Thayer, one of my best patients. He sprained his ankle pretty badly, but I've never seen anyone so motivated to get better." She smiled at the tall man. "And this is my friend Harry, and his friend Charles. Charles is the boy I told you about. His family is taking care of Cocoa."

"Ah!" said the judge. He had a kind face, Charles thought, with blue-sky eyes and a crooked smile. He stuck out a long, thin hand for a shake. It reminded Charles of the long, thin gray branches of the old apple tree in his yard. "Call me Ernest. I bet Cocoa is running you ragged, isn't she?"

Charles laughed. "She's a terrific dog," he said. "She sure does have a lot of energy, though." He looked at the judge, so tall and skinny and gray, and wondered how he could possibly manage such a wild puppy.

"Well, what do we have here?" A small, thin older woman walked over to pet Zeke. "Land sakes, if this dog doesn't look just like Cocoa."

"This is my wife, Charlotte," said the judge.

If the judge was like an old apple tree, thought Charles, his wife was like a little bird sitting in one of the branches. She was tiny — no taller than Herbie Klotz, the tallest boy in Charles's class. And she was old and gray, just like the judge. But she had bright eyes, just like a bird's, and a pretty voice.

Harry introduced Charlotte to Zeke. She shook the big dog's paw and smiled. "You're a lot calmer than our Cocoa, aren't you?" She turned to Charles. "I hope your family is surviving our wild puppy."

Charles smiled. "She's great. She's just a little" — he didn't want to say "hyper," which was what Mom had called her — "full of energy, that's all," he finished.

Charlotte nodded in agreement. "She's been that way all along, ever since our son gave her to us last year as a Christmas present. We always had Labs when he was a boy, and he thought it would be fun for us to have one now. But goodness, we do have a little trouble keeping up with her!"

Zeke, who had been waiting patiently for more attention, held up a paw for the judge to shake.

"Hey, there," said the judge, stooping over to take Zeke's paw. "Now, you're a mature one, aren't you?" He stood back up. "We have a neighbor boy who walks Cocoa every day after school, but I'm afraid it just isn't enough. She has a lot of bottled-up excitement. Poor thing."

"You're not mad that she hurt your leg?" Charles asked.

The judge laughed. "How could anybody be mad at Cocoa for long? Anyway, it really wasn't her fault. She's just young and, as you said, full of energy." He looked thoughtful for a moment. "Two things that I am *not* anymore, I'm afraid."

"Oh, Judge," said Dawna. "You know what they say. You're only as old as you feel." She smiled at him as she helped him step up and down and up again.

"Well, in that case I guess I must be about a hundred and fifty," said the judge, smiling back at her.

Later, on the way home, it was snowing hard. Charles and Harry did not talk much as they rode in the red convertible. Instead, Harry peered through the windshield as he drove, slowly and carefully, back to Charles's house. "Tomorrow's my day off from work, and Dawna's, too. Looks like we might be able to have a team practice," he said, when he pulled up in front. "If you get a snow day, that is."

A snow day! Charles grinned. It had been a long time since school had closed because of too much snow. Then his smile faded. Would he really be able to cross-country ski well enough to be on Harry's team? He hoped he would not embarrass himself in front of Harry and Dawna — not to mention the whole town.

CHAPTER SEVEN

Snow day! Charles knew it as soon as he woke up the next morning. He could tell by the quiet, muffled sounds from outside like the scrape of snow shovels. There were no traffic noises, just the beeping of a snowplow backing up. He jumped out of bed and ran to the window. Sure enough, snow had fallen all night long, leaving a thick white blanket covering everything in sight. A few flakes still drifted down.

"Snow day!" he said to Buddy and Cocoa. They stretched and yawned on the rug next to his bed, where they had slept all curled up next to each other.

"Snow day!" said Lizzie, popping into the room. "Mom just checked online. All the schools are closed. Yahoo!" She opened her arms wide to let Cocoa jump up on her, and they waltzed around together. "Want to go sledding? I'm going to call Maria and tell her to meet me at the school."

Sledding sounded great — but Charles had other things on his mind. "I have to practice my skiing," he said. "For the relay race." He wasn't even sure where his skis were, but hopefully Mom could help him find them.

It seemed like hours before they were ready to go: first there was breakfast, then there was getting dressed, including stuffing the Bean into his snowsuit and boots from last year (which didn't fit so well anymore) then finding the skis, then loading all the sleds and skis — and two puppies — into the van. Charles got covered with snow as he helped Dad shovel the driveway, and had to change into a different jacket and find his other mittens. But finally, they were on their way, singing *"Deck the halls with bells of jolly"* as Mom drove.

As they neared the school, Charles could see that the sledding hill was packed. Dozens of kids — and grown-ups, too — were sliding down and climbing back up. Their jackets and hats made splotches of bright color against the white snow. "Mom, can you drop me off over on the other side?" Charles asked. "I want to practice skiing on the flat part." Flat — and private. Charles didn't want anyone watching him until he remembered how the whole skiing thing worked. Harry and Dawna would be arriving soon for a team practice — Harry had called that morning to make a plan — but Charles knew he needed to practice on his own first.

"Let's drop Lizzie off," Mom said. "Then the Bean and I will come watch you." She had brought the Bean's sled to tow him around on.

"Buddy can come with me," Lizzie said. "He's always good around the sledders. He never barks or chases."

"Okay," said Mom. "As long as you keep an eye on him. And we'll take Cocoa."

Charles watched a little wistfully as Lizzie ran to join Maria. He loved sledding, and he could see his friends Sammy and David racing each other down the hill. But if he was going to be part of Rudolph's Revenge, he had to practice his skiing.

Mom parked over by the running track, and Charles unloaded his skis and set them on the snow. He leaned on his ski poles as he pushed the toes of his boots into one binding and then the other. *Click. Click.* Done! Charles stood up straight, smiling and ready to go. Then he fell — *splat!* — onto his back.

Cocoa bounded over, towing Mom through the snow, and began to lick Charles's face all over.

Want some kisses?

"Cocoa!" Charles pushed her away. "Not now." But he couldn't help laughing. Cocoa was always in such a good mood. And at least Harry and Dawna had not arrived yet, so only Mom and the Bean had seen his not-very-graceful fall. He grabbed on to Cocoa's collar and leaned on her to help himself up. Then he got himself arranged again and slipped his hands through his pole straps.

As Mom got the Bean tucked into his sled, Charles took a first few tentative steps on his skis. Kick, glide, kick, glide. He remembered Dad teaching him how to ski, that first time up in

Vermont. He fell again, and picked himself up again. Kick, glide, kick, glide. Then, suddenly, he was doing it! He found his balance and began to slide over the snow, his arms and legs finding their own rhythm.

"Look, Mom!" he yelled. "I'm doing it. I can ski!"

"Great!" she called. She followed him around the track, pulling the Bean in his sled as Cocoa dragged her along from the front. "I'm in a one-horse open sleigh!" the Bean yelled. "You're my horsie, Mommy!"

Charles laughed.

Then he fell again.

Cocoa dragged Mom over to where Charles lay. "Are you okay?" Mom asked.

"I'm fine," said Charles, struggling to his feet. His skis got all tangled with his poles and he almost went down again. Falling wasn't so bad — it was the getting-up part that was hard.

Soon he was back up and skiing. "Go, Charles!" Mom yelled. "Looking good!"

"Yay, Charles!" shouted the Bean. "Bells of jolly!"

Then Cocoa started to bark. She barked louder and louder, dragging Mom faster and faster along the track. "Help!" Mom yelled. "I can't hold her!"

What was the big brown pup barking at? Charles looked toward the parking lot and saw two people walking toward them. Harry and Dawna!

Charles glanced back just in time to see Cocoa pull the leash right out of Mom's hand. She came charging toward Charles, on her way to greet the newcomers. Loose dog! Without thinking, Charles threw down his ski poles and grabbed the end of her leash as she galloped by. With a jerk, he felt the powerful dog begin to tow him along, and his skis hummed through the snow. He was going faster than he had ever gone on his own. For a second he was scared. But only for a second. This was way more fun than sledding. "Wheee!" he yelled. Somehow, he managed to stay upright.

"Better let her go!" yelled Harry. "We'll catch her."

Charles let go of the leash. He glided to a stop as Cocoa charged ahead, straight for Harry. "Got her!" yelled Harry, as he grabbed the leash. He and Dawna laughed and hooted as Cocoa jumped and twirled and barked.

"Whoa, Charles," said Dawna, as he skiied up to them. "That was awesome. Harry said you could ski, but I didn't know you could skijor!"

CHAPTER EIGHT

Charles stood panting, trying to catch his breath, while Cocoa danced around Harry and Dawna, leaping up to kiss their noses.

Hi, hi, hi! I know you! It's always great to see friends!

"Skijor?" Charles asked finally, when he could speak again. "I don't even know what that is, much less how to do it."

"Skijoring is a sport that started in Scandinavia. It's sort of like dogsledding, only instead of the dog pulling a sled, the dog is pulling you — on skis," Dawna told him, as she petted Cocoa and rubbed her ears. "A friend of mine does it every winter. She loves it. Of course, you can't really do it the way you were, with a regular leash and collar. That wouldn't be safe for the dog. You need a special type of harness. Isn't that right, Cocoa?" She scratched Cocoa's head and Cocoa grinned her happy dog grin.

"Hey, maybe you could borrow Cocoa and try it out," Harry said to Dawna. "She'd probably be great at skijoring, since she loves to pull."

"You'd be more than welcome to," Mom said. She had finally caught up to them, towing the Bean on his sled. When she panted, big puffs of white frosty breath hung in the cold, still air. "This puppy needs more exercise than any puppy we've ever fostered."

"Deck the halls with bells of jolly," sang the

Bean from his seat on the sled. He flashed Harry and Dawna his cutest smile, the one with dimples.

Harry and Dawna both giggled. "That is adorable," said Dawna.

"Not if you've heard it a billion times," Charles muttered, but he had to admit that the Bean looked pretty cute, all zipped up in his bunny rabbit snowsuit with his ever-present antlers perched atop his hood.

"I think I'll take the Bean home," Mom said to Charles, "now that Harry and Dawna are here. He could use an N-A-P."

"No! No!" yelled the Bean. "Don't want to nap!" He started to cry.

Mom rolled her eyes. "I guess he learned what N-A-P spells."

"If you go home with Mom" — Charles leaned down to whisper to his little brother — "I'll help you write your letter to Santa later. How about that?"

The Bean stopped crying for a moment and squinted up at him. "Okay," he said finally. He waved his arms at Mom. "Let's go, horsie!" Then he began to sing again. *"Deck the halls with bells of jolly!"*

Mom rolled her eyes again, but she gave Charles a grateful smile. "I'll come back to pick you and Lizzie up in an hour or so," she said as she trudged off, towing the Bean on his sled.

"Hey," Harry said to Charles, "you're looking pretty good on those skis!"

Charles looked down at his feet. He'd almost forgotten that he still had his skis on. He smiled at Harry. "Thanks," he said. "I guess I remembered how to do it."

"Rudolph's Revenge is going to *rule!*" said Harry,

grinning as he gave Charles a fist bump. "This race is going to be so much fun."

"I hope Judge Thayer can be there to see us," said Dawna. She turned to Charles. "That's the goal he and I agreed on yesterday. He's tired of the rehab center. I made him a deal: if he can walk well enough with a cane or ski pole so that he can come to WinterFest, then he can go home and finish his rehab there, with visits from me."

"Won't it be hard for him to walk on the snow?" Charles asked.

"They clear the paths pretty well," Dawna said. "But actually, that's part of the point. I can't send someone home in winter if they can't get around on ice and snow."

Charles nodded. Wow. Judge Thayer was getting better fast. Soon he and Charlotte were going to want to have Cocoa back. There was only one problem: Charles was beginning to wonder if that was a good idea. He had been thinking about it a lot, ever since he had met Judge Thayer and his wife.

The thing was, when his family fostered puppies, their goal was to find each puppy a home. Not just any home, but the best possible forever home. Big puppies, little puppies, timid puppies, mischievous puppies: each one had his or her own personality. And for each personality, there was someone who was ready to love that puppy and give it a wonderful life.

Charles felt terrible to even *think* it, but he was just not sure that Ernest and Charlotte Thayer were Cocoa's perfect forever family. Cocoa was an active, energetic dog who needed to be on the go for hours every single day. She needed to learn some manners, but it was going to be easy to teach her anything until she calmed down a little bit. She was a handful, just as Harry had predicted. Maybe she was just too much for two very old, frail people.

But Charles didn't know how to say so. How could he, just a little kid, ask someone to give up a dog they adored?

"I wonder how Judge Thayer and his wife will feel when they see Cocoa," Charles said. He saw Harry and Dawna exchange a look.

"I'm sure they'll be very happy to see her," said Dawna. "But . . ." She didn't finish her sentence.

Harry looked down at the ground and nodded. Charles could tell that Harry and Dawna were thinking the same thoughts he was. "But the judge may have a major decision to make," said Harry. "Not about whether someone in his courtroom is guilty or not, but about whether he and Charlotte will be able to keep Cocoa."

All three of them were quiet for a moment.

Then Cocoa sat back on her haunches and barked.

Hey, I thought we were going to have some fun *here today!*

The serious mood was broken. Charles, Harry, and Dawna all cracked up. "Okay, okay," Harry said. "You're right, Cocoa. It's time for some running and playing, isn't it?" He reached for the sled he had propped next to him.

Dawna knelt down to strap on her snowshoes, giggling as Cocoa licked her face.

And Charles skied back to find his poles.

It was time for Rudolph's Revenge to prepare for the big race.

Charles was tired that night after practice, but he had made a promise to his little brother. After dinner, Charles helped the Bean write his letter to Santa. Then he wrote a quick note of his own. *Dear Santa,* it said. *There are a few things I'd like for Christmas, but more about those later. The most important thing I want is for Cocoa to find the perfect forever home. And I think I may know just where that might be. . . .*

CHAPTER NINE

It snowed again on Friday night, just enough to freshen everything with a new layer of white. Saturday morning was sunny and bright. Charles bounded down the stairs with Cocoa and Buddy flying behind him. "It's a perfect day for Winter-Fest!" he said, as he sat down at the breakfast table.

"And a perfect day for blueberry pancakes," said Dad, smiling as he handed Charles a heaping plateful. "Eat up. You'll need all your energy for your big race today."

Charles looked down at Cocoa. Was it a perfect day for her to go back to her owners? He wondered again what would happen when Judge

Thayer saw his dog for the first time. Would the judge and his wife want to take Cocoa home today?

"Deck the halls with bells of jolly," sang the Bean, prancing around the kitchen in his antlers. *"Fa la la la la, la la la la!"*

Charles laughed, pushing away his worried thoughts.

Dad sighed and shook his head. "I used to *like* that song," he said. But he was still smiling. "Hey, look what I found at the dollar store last night." He handed Charles a big shopping bag.

Charles peeked inside. "Antlers!" he said.

Dad beamed. "Enough for all your fans," he said. "Rudolph's Revenge will have a whole *herd* of reindeer cheering them on."

The school grounds were already packed by the time Charles and his family arrived at WinterFest. Charles looked around. He did not see Judge

Thayer, but there were Harry and Dawna, their antlers bobbing above the crowd. He waved to them, then turned to pull his skis out of the van. He had to laugh when he looked at his family: Mom, Dad, the Bean, and Lizzie, all wearing antlers. Plus, Dad still had a whole bunch more to hand out to anyone who wanted to support Rudolph's Revenge.

The relay race was one of the last events of the day, so Charles set his skis aside and took Cocoa for a walk around the playground. He had put a head harness on her, so she walked nicely next to him without pulling as they explored the winter carnival that had sprung up overnight. There were snow sculptures: dragons and giant Viking boats and castles with fluttering banners, and, in the middle of the baseball field, a huge pile of wood all ready to be lit for the evening bonfire. A network of paths, carefully shoveled and sanded, connected everything.

"Hey, look, Cocoa," said Charles. "The snowmen

are already done." A row of blank-faced snowmen stretched along one edge of the field. They were part of the relay race this year. Harry had explained it all during their practice.

The way the race worked was this: When each sledder got to the bottom of the steep hill, he or she would run to one of the snowmen and put a scarf around its neck. As soon as the scarf was on, the snowshoer would run around the track, then use a handful of pebbles to add a mouth and two eyes to the snowman's face. As soon as that was done, the snowshoer would run up to the skier, waiting at the top of another, less steep hill. The skier would ski down to add the final touch to the snowman: a carrot nose. The first team to complete their snowman won the race.

Charles patted his pocket, looking for the carrot he'd brought from home, and looked up toward the long, gentle hill he would be skiing down. He felt his heart skip a beat. He was still a little nervous about the race, but after all the practicing he was as ready as he'd ever be. "No problem, right, Cocoa?" he asked. Cocoa grinned up at him and wagged her tail.

Right!

"Cocoa! The famous Cocoa. I've been hearing so much about you!"

It was Dee. Her wheelchair was strapped onto a toboggan and a crew of "elves" (actually some of Harry's teammates from the basketball team) in pointy green hats hauled her across the snow. She wore a sparkly crown and a sash that proclaimed her "Queen of WinterFest." Murphy, her beautiful chocolate Lab, trotted along beside her, keeping an eye on everything.

Hearing her name, Cocoa pulled hard on her leash and dragged Charles over to Dee. She and Murphy sniffed at each other, tails wagging.

"Hello, Your Majesty," said Charles, bowing down before Dee.

Dee grinned. "My staff made me wear this," she said. She scratched Cocoa's ears. "Harry was right. This pup is a real cutie. She'd be perfect for Daw —" She stopped and put her hand over her mouth. "Forget I said that. I know Cocoa belongs to someone." She changed the subject. "What do you think of WinterFest?"

"I think it's great," said Charles. He had a feeling he knew what Dee had been about to say. "I can't wait to try snowball bingo and check out the hot cocoa stand."

"And the tug-of-war should be beginning soon," said Dee. "But of course the main event is the relay race. Did you know that between the four teams you've already raised over two thousand dollars for people who can't afford to heat their homes this winter?" She waved a stack of pledge forms at him.

Charles was surprised. "I didn't even know that the race was a fund-raiser," he admitted. "But that's great."

"I bet Harry and Dawna didn't want you to worry about collecting pledges, since you're so busy taking care of Cocoa," said Dee. "But there are a lot of people out there who will be warmer this winter, and you're part of that."

The whole time they'd been talking, Cocoa had been trying to get Murphy to play. But as a service dog, he was trained not to play during work hours. After that first sniff hello, he sat like a statue, barely flicking an ear, while Cocoa danced around him. Finally, she sat down and began to bark.

This is frustrating! Why won't you wrestle? I know you like to have fun.

Charles and Dee laughed. "I'd better keep this pup moving," said Charles. He waved to Dee as he and Cocoa set off across the field. It was time to find Sammy and David and check out some of the games.

Later, as the afternoon shadows began to fall, Charles stood at the top of the hill, wearing his skis, his heart pounding as he waited for the race to begin. Any minute now, Dee would call "ready, set, go" over the loudspeaker, and Harry would flop down on his sled. And soon after that, Dawna would finish her snowshoe run, make the snowman smile, and tag Charles. He checked his pocket again for the carrot, then scanned the crowd, wondering if Judge Thayer would make it in time to see the race. He spotted Mom, who was holding Cocoa's leash. Dad stood next to her, carrying the Bean piggyback. There was Lizzie with her friend Maria, with Buddy sitting between them. But where was Judge Thayer?

Wait — who was that, picking his way carefully along one of the paths? A tall, thin man with a limp, leaning on a ski pole. A tiny woman walked beside him. The judge and his wife had arrived.

CHAPTER TEN

It seemed to take forever for the race to start. Charles thought he would jump out of his skin waiting to hear Dee say "go." He bent down to tighten his ski boot laces, then stood up again, wobbling a bit on his skis. Would he be able to ski fast enough? Would he crash in front of everyone? Time seemed to slow down as Charles waited. But once the race began, it all went by in a blur. Charles saw Harry fly down the hill on his sled and wrap the scarf around the snowman's neck. He watched Dawna charge around the track on her snowshoes and add the pebbles to the snowman's face. Then she ran up to him and he felt her tap his arm, the signal that it was his turn. At that moment, his worries fell away and his body took over as he let his skis glide fast, faster, faster over the snow, carrying him straight down to the snowman. He came to a stop just at the right spot, plunged his hand into his pocket to pull out the carrot, and stuck it into the middle of the snowman's face.

"Yay!" he yelled, throwing his arms into the air. He had no idea if his team had won — that didn't even matter. All that mattered was that they had finished, and that he had not embarrassed his team or himself by falling flat on his face.

"Whoo-hoo! Charles!" He saw his family running toward him, all wearing their antlers. Lizzie could barely hold Cocoa back as she lunged forward, wearing her huge doggy grin.

Oh, boy, oh, boy! Now I get to run!

"Yes!" shouted Harry, as he and Dawna ran over to join Charles. "Great job, man!" He smacked

Charles a big high five as Dawna knelt to throw her arms around Cocoa.

In a happy daze, Charles glanced around at the crowd and saw Judge Thayer looking straight back at him. Well, not at him, exactly. The judge stared at Dawna and Cocoa, who were now wrestling happily on the snow. Charles had never seen someone look so happy and so sad at the same time.

Charles nudged Dawna and pointed to the judge and Charlotte, who were now working their way toward them. Dawna nodded and tightened her hold on Cocoa. "I know you'll be excited to see them," she told the dog. "But you can't jump up, okay?" Cocoa wagged her tail.

She wagged even harder when she spotted her owners.

"Good girl," said Judge Thayer, leaning on his crutch and reaching out one long, thin hand to pet Cocoa's head. He smiled at Charles. "She looks terrific. I can tell your family's been taking good care of her." Cocoa gazed up at the judge lovingly as he stroked her ears.

"She's a great dog," Charles said.

"You're absolutely right about that," said the judge. "But —"

Just then, Dee's voice came over the loudspeaker. "It's time to light the bonfire and announce the winners of our relay race. Please, everyone, join us for hot cocoa and singing."

The Bean jumped up and down, his antlers bobbing. "Time to sing! Time to sing! Come on!" He grabbed Charles's hand and started to drag him away. Charles looked back helplessly at the judge, who was leaning over again to pet Cocoa.

Later, Charles stood near the hot, crackling bonfire listening to the Bean's class sing, a hot mug of cocoa cupped in his hands. Mom came over and put her hands on his shoulders. "Congrat- ulations," she whispered into his ear. "I heard Dee announce that Rudolph's Revenge won the race."

Charles beamed up at her.

"I've invited everyone back to our house for Chinese food," she told him. "Harry and Dee, Dawna, Judge Thayer and his wife. I'm going to stop by and pick up the food. Dad will bring you home in a little while."

"Yay!" said Charles. "Can you get me some House Special chow fun?"

At home, Charles took Cocoa and Buddy out into the backyard for a good run before they all sat down to eat. Would this be one of the last times he got to throw the ball for Cocoa? As he watched Cocoa run and chase, he knew in his heart that this pup needed an owner who could keep up with her. The only problem was how to convince Judge and Charlotte Thayer of that.

Charles threw the ball five more times, and Cocoa fetched it five times, racing ahead of Buddy. Then he headed back inside with both dogs. "Wait!" he said, as he opened the back door. Buddy waited. Cocoa did not. She charged into the house, straight for a group of people standing in the kitchen: Dawna and Harry, talking to the judge, who balanced on his crutches as he drank from a mug.

"Oh, no!" Charles watched in horror as Cocoa barreled toward them. But the puppy did not run to Judge Thayer. She headed straight for Dawna and skidded to a stop as Dawna bent down to meet her.

"Okay, there, girl," Dawna murmured to the big pup as she stroked her. "Easy, now. Let's calm down and take it easy."

Charles looked at the judge. The tall man wore that same happy-sad expression Charles had seen at WinterFest.

It was time to clear the air. "Judge Thayer," Charles asked, "are you going to take Cocoa home soon?"

"Charlotte and I have been talking about that," said the judge slowly. "We love Cocoa very much, but we know she is really too much dog for us to handle. We think Cocoa deserves a home with someone who can keep up with her." The judge looked straight at Dawna. "Someone like Dawna. When we saw her run into your arms after your relay race, we just knew. Our beloved Cocoa belongs with you."

"Really?" asked Dawna, straightening up. She smiled. "I would love to give Cocoa a home. But only if you promise that I can bring her to visit you when I come to your home to help you finish up your physical therapy. And when you're all healed, we'd still want to visit as often as you'd like. What do you say?"

Judge Thayer and Charlotte looked at each other, nodded, and smiled. "I'd say that sounds perfect," said Judge Thayer.

Charles noticed that the judge looked more happy and less sad as they all watched Dawna hug Cocoa. He knew it could not be easy for the judge and Charlotte to give up their beautiful dog — but he also knew that it was the right decision.

"Wonderful," said Mom, setting the last of the platters of food on the table. "Now that we've got that settled, why don't we eat?"

Harry sat next to Charles at the table. "A pretty good day all around, wouldn't you say?" Harry asked. "And now I get to sit with one of my favorite people and eat my favorite dish from China Star." He reached for the platter of House Special chow fun. "You know," he said, "I never really had a favorite there and I always wanted one. Then I overheard you ordering this, so I tried it. It's great! Mind if we have the same favorite?"

"Not at all," said Charles, grinning as Harry passed him the platter. "Not at all."

PUPPY TIPS

An energetic dog like Cocoa can be a real handful, but there are ways to help a rambunctious puppy calm down. Try to stay calm yourself; if you squeal and raise your hands, the puppy is more likely to jump up on you. If you stand still and just turn away if she does jump, it will help her learn that jumping is not okay. Pet your puppy with long, easy strokes and speak in a low, soothing voice. Take your dog to puppy kindergarten or dog-training classes. Puppies aren't born with good manners — they need to learn them. Plus, the trainer there will have lots more ideas to help you deal with your wild child.

Dear Reader,

I have a fan named Sarah who writes once in a while to tell me about her puppy Toby and all his adventures. She gives me updates on everything from the day she first brought him home, to his first collar, to his first Christmas. Toby is a chocolate Lab just like Cocoa (Toby is short for Toblerone, a kind of candy bar), and he is full of mischief. He likes to chew up his own doggy beds, play with his toys, and race around with his dog friends. Once he jumped into the fish pond at a friend's house! Luckily, Sarah is in a 4-H club where she does a lot of dog training, so I bet Toby will grow up to be a very well-behaved dog.

Yours from the Puppy Place,
Ellen Miles

P.S. For another sweetheart of a puppy, check out SWEETIE.

THE PUPPY PLACE

DON'T MISS THE NEXT PUPPY PLACE ADVENTURE!

Here's a peek at ROCKY!

Lizzie caught her breath and took a closer look. *Free Puppy* the ad said. *Bulldog.* Then there was a phone number. That was all.

She frowned. Why didn't it say *To a Good Home*? It sounded like the person was just going to give the puppy to the first person who called. That was no good. Ms. Dobbins, the director of the local animal shelter where Lizzie volunteered every week, would never do that. If someone wanted to adopt a pet from Caring Paws, they had to fill out a long application with lots of information about who they were, where they lived, and how they planned to take care of the animal that was about to become part of their family. Ms. Dobbins didn't just let anyone walk in, pay the adoption fee, and walk back out with a cat or dog.

Lizzie's aunt Amanda, who ran a doggy daycare center where Lizzie sometimes helped out, would have agreed. She had told Lizzie that responsible dog breeders never sold puppies without interviewing buyers first.

Lizzie thought for a second. Then she closed the notebook in which she'd been writing her pen pal letter. She picked up the newspaper and pushed back her chair. "Mom," she yelled.

Buddy scrabbled to his feet and followed her out of the kitchen and up the stairs.

"Mom," Lizzie said again as she walked into her mother's study.

Mom spun around on her office chair and

rubbed her eyes. "What is it, honey?" she asked. She looked tired. Mom had been working hard lately on a series of articles about older people in the community. So far she had interviewed a farmer, a husband-and-wife team who ran a flower shop, and a retired detective. She said she loved the project, but Lizzie had noticed that she often went back into her study late at night, instead of reading or watching a movie in the living room.

"Mom, look at this ad," Lizzie said, plopping the paper down on her mother's lap.

Mom picked it up and studied the classifieds. "Which one?" she asked. "The one where someone's selling a saltwater aquarium? I don't think we —"

"No, this one," said Lizzie, pointing to the ad.

"Aha," said Mom. "Well. I hope they find the puppy a good home."

"Exactly," said Lizzie. "That's exactly my point. It doesn't even look like they're trying!" She picked up the paper. "It's like they don't care *who* takes the puppy."

Mom nodded. "That's too bad," she said.

"Mom?" Lizzie asked. She came over to lean on her mom's chair. Buddy joined her, leaning against Mom's legs.

"Oh, no, Lizzie. You're not thinking —" Mom started to shake her head.

"I am," said Lizzie. "I think we should foster this puppy."